CARL JUNG ON SYNCHRONICITY

WHY UNIVERSE IS A LIVING ORGANISM & EVERYTHING IS CONNECTED?

SOM DUTT

Made with ♥ on the Notion Press Platform
www.notionpress.com

To Dionysus,

The enigmatic deity who has stirred the depths of my soul and opened the gates to realms unknown, This book is dedicated to you, Dionysus, the god of wine, dance, music, chaos, intoxication, ecstasy, and divine madness. You have whispered in my dreams and inspired me to see the world through a kaleidoscope of perspectives, urging me to embrace the hidden truths and untamed passions that dwell within.

You, Dionysus, have been both muse and tormentor, guiding me on a tumultuous journey where reason and rationality melt away, leaving room for the wild and the extraordinary. Through your intoxicating influence, you have unveiled the masks we wear, inviting me to question conventions, challenge boundaries, and immerse myself in the untamed beauty of existence.

In the depths of the night, your spirit dances with mine, blurring the lines between reality and madness, inviting me to taste the fruits of life with reckless abandon. You haunt me with visions that sear into my unconsciousness, coaxing me to unravel the mysteries of existence, to seek truth in the shadows, and to embrace the contradictions that define our humanity.

Oh, Dionysus, you are the god of awakening, and liberation, the shatterer of constraints, and the revealer of the hidden. You have shown me that life is a masquerade, and that to truly live, one must shed the inhibitions that bind us and surrender to the ecstasy of the unknown.

Through this book, I endeavor to capture the essence of your intoxicating spirit, to share with the world the transformative power of embracing the multifaceted nature of our existence. May it serve as an invitation to others to embark on their own journeys of self-discovery, personal growth, and revelation, guided by the wisdom and chaos that you embody.

To Dionysus, the god who inspires and haunts me in my dreams, I offer my eternal gratitude and this humble tribute. In wine, in dance, and in ecstatic reverie, we shall forever celebrate the magic you bestow.

" ***"Sometimes, things want to be done but to be done only through you."***

Som Dutt "

Contents

Prologue

As a top writer on psychology and philosophy on Medium.com, synchronicity has profoundly impacted Som Dutt's intellectual, personal journey to perceive the interconnectedness of unrelated events, offering a richer and more nuanced understanding of the human experience.

He is convinced that these synchronistic events bridge the gap between the subjective inner world and the objective external reality, providing us with profound insights and personal growth. These archetypal patterns, deeply embedded in the collective unconscious, shape our thoughts, emotions, and behaviors when an individual's inner psychic state resonates with an external event, resulting in a meaningful connection.

These connections can manifest as dreams, symbols, and even encounters with specific individuals. By recognizing and engaging with synchronistic events, individuals can gain valuable insights into their unconscious desires, unresolved conflicts, and untapped potentials. Such experiences act as guideposts along the path of self-discovery and deepening our connection with the broader fabric of existence.

Preface

In a world where everything seems to be governed by chance and randomness, the concept of synchronicity holds a captivating allure. It is an idea that transcends the boundaries of conventional logic, revealing the hidden connections between our inner and outer worlds. This book, "Carl Jung on Synchronicity," aims to delve into the profound wisdom and insights of the renowned Swiss psychologist, Carl Gustav Jung, as he explored the enigmatic realm of synchronicity.

I found myself drawn to this subject matter not only because of its intellectual intrigue but also because of its potential to profoundly transform our understanding of reality. As I delved into Jung's writings and studies, I discovered a vast reservoir of wisdom that resonated deeply with my own experiences and observations. This book is the culmination of my journey to unravel the intricate tapestry of synchronicity and to share its profound implications with a wider audience.

Inspiration for this book came not only from Jung's groundbreaking work but also from my own encounters with synchronistic events. I have witnessed the inexplicable coincidences that seem to defy rational explanations. These instances, when seemingly unrelated events align with uncanny precision, leave an indelible imprint on our consciousness. They invite us to question the fabric of reality and consider the existence of a deeper, interconnected web of meaning.

Through this book, I seek to invite readers into a profound exploration of synchronicity, encouraging them to examine their own experiences and ponder the hidden forces that shape their lives. I believe that the insights contained within these pages will resonate with individuals from all walks of life, for synchronicity knows no boundaries. It touches us in our relationships, career choices, creative endeavors, and even in the realm of spirituality.

By delving into the timeless wisdom of Carl Jung and blending it with contemporary perspectives, I hope to shed light on the significance of synchronicity in our modern lives. This book is a humble attempt to bridge the gap between theory and personal experience, offering practical tools and guidance to help readers navigate the intricacies of synchronistic encounters and embrace the transformative power they hold.

After publishing more than 500 articles on Philosophy and Psychology on Medium.com. I was convinced that Nietzsche's thoughts has a huge influence on Jung. Therefore I started to dig into Jung deeply. Then on 1st January 2023, I have written a Blog article as "Carj Jung on Synchronicity" and it became a kind of viral to me. Still, this article is ranked on the first page of Google. But this is not the case with my inspiration. After meeting Michelle, I started getting lots of clues on Synchronicity and found that the Universal Want is talking to us. I was totally against such phenomena because they do not have any logical explanation but when I started observing them first hand I started to dig deep into the subject.

In March 2023, I started to write on it and it eventually turned out to be a manuscript of more than 70000 words and I was shocked. I took so many breaks and started editing it. It took me almost 1 month to edit it. I do not want to edit it in one go. Therefore I was doing it slowly and enjoying the process. There were a few incidences where

I was thinking to convert this book into a series of articles because of its monetization benefits. Then I have convinced that this manuscript is destined to be a Book. And I did not care about the money part as I usually do. I always chose my creativity and Universal Want over money.

I am convinced that many people will find themselves deeply connected to the ideas presented here. Synchronicity has an innate capacity to awaken a sense of wonder and mystery within us, allowing us to tap into a deeper understanding of our existence. Whether you are a curious seeker, a psychology enthusiast, or simply someone intrigued by the mysteries of life, this book offers a rich tapestry of knowledge that will both captivate and illuminate.

Prepare to embark on a journey into the realm of synchronicity, where the threads of meaning weave together to create a tapestry of interconnectedness. As you turn each page, may you open your mind to the awe-inspiring beauty of synchronicity and embrace the possibility that there is more to our world than meets the eye.

Welcome to the world of Carl Jung on Synchronicity.

Acknowledgements

I would like to begin by expressing my deepest gratitude to the mysterious workings of the Universal Want, which have guided me on this remarkable journey of understanding synchronicity, quantum entanglement, and the profound significance of number synchronicities. In contemplating the intricate tapestry of existence, I have come to recognize these phenomena as enigmatic clues given by a higher power—an expression of divine orchestration.

To all those who have contemplated the mysteries of life, sought meaning in the seemingly random events that unfold before us, and dared to embrace the notion that there is a deeper connection between the seen and the unseen, I extend my sincerest appreciation. Your openness, curiosity, and unwavering belief in the power of synchronicity have inspired my exploration and fueled my conviction.

I am indebted to the great minds who have ventured into the realms of quantum mechanics, unraveling the intricate dance of particles and unveiling the entangled nature of our reality. Their tireless pursuit of knowledge has paved the way for a deeper understanding of the interconnectedness that permeates the cosmos.

Additionally, I would like to acknowledge Michelle Mariscal who has shared her personal experiences of synchronicity and number synchronicities with me. Your stories have illuminated the profound impact these occurrences can have on our lives, providing glimpses of guidance, validation, and spiritual awakening. Your courage in embracing these signs has been a testament to the transformative power of synchronicity.

Furthermore, I am grateful to the teachings of ancient wisdom traditions, spiritual leaders, and mystics such as Carl Jung and Friedrich Nietzsche who have long recognized the significance of synchronicity in the human journey. Their insights and profound wisdom continue to inspire and shape our understanding of these extraordinary phenomena.

As we embark upon this exploration of synchronicity, quantum entanglement, and the intricacies of number synchronicities, let us remain open to the possibilities that lie before us. May we embrace the profound implications these phenomena hold for our understanding of ourselves, our place in the universe, and the eternal connection that binds us all.

Foreword

"The importance of Jung's discovery bears considering. Since the seventeenth century, we've been taught that what is "in our heads" is only "subjective," that we are all island universes, separate worlds, and that everything in those worlds has been furnished with material taken from outside, from the senses, as if our minds began as empty rooms, waiting for the mental equivalent of a trip to Ikea. Yet anyone, like myself, who has had precognitive dreams or experienced synchronicities or telepathy or other "paranormal" phenomena knows this isn't quite true. Jung knew this and is saying that there are things in our heads that have nothing to do with us or our senses. In his book Heaven and Hell Aldous Huxley made the same point. "Like the earth of a hundred years ago," Huxley wrote, "our mind still has its darkest Africas, its unmapped Borneos and Amazonian basins." And while the creatures that inhabit these "far continents" of the mind seem "improbable," they are nevertheless "facts of observation," which argues for their "complete autonomy" and "self-sufficiency."18 Huxley borrowed the title of his book from another extraordinary inner explorer, the Swedish sage Emanuel Swedenborg, who was a powerful influence on Jung, and who, like Jung, was a practiced hypnagogist and developed a method of entering similar inner worlds."
— Gary Valentine Lachman, Jung the Mystic: The Esoteric Dimensions of Carl Jung's Life & Teachings

CHAPTER I

The Introduction

Carl Jung (1875–1961) was born in Switzerland and became interested in philosophy at an early age. He studied medicine at Basel University but never practiced medicine; instead, he focused on his studies of philosophy and psychology—the latter being his true passion. He founded analytical psychology and developed an influential theory of personality, which centered on the significance of the unconscious in human behavior.

> "*Synchronicity is an ever present reality for those who have eyes to see.*
> *— Carl Jung*"

He is renowned for his work in dream analysis and developing the concepts of archetypes, extraversion, and introversion. He also made important contributions to dream analysis and to the study of the collective unconscious. He argued that our unconscious mind is always trying to communicate something important to us, but we're often too distracted by daily life to notice it.

His philosophy is mainly based on two principles: meaningfulness and acausal connection (synchronicity). Meaningfulness refers to the idea that there is order in the world, even though we may not always be able to perceive it; acausal connections are events that seem related but cannot be explained by cause-and-effect logic.

Through synchronicities, an internal process or inner necessity is seeking expression. He always thought that there is a constant conversation going on between you and the universe. The Universe is an alive Organism and all events are connected by an underlying pattern or structure in space-time (the "collective unconscious").

In other words, he thought there was an underlying order to life itself—a sort of universal mind at work behind the scenes influencing everything we do and experience every day. And sometimes it can be wrongly taken as confirmation biases and meaning is a very subjective thing. Because the universe is just a creation of the mind.

> "*Synchronicity is the coming together of inner and outer events in a way that cannot be explained by cause and effect and that is meaningful to the observer.*
> *— Carl Jung*"

These encounters are not haphazard but rather show us something important about ourselves and our world. Therefore these moments reveal some connection between our own minds and the larger universe (like a universal mind) around us—a connection he called "the collective unconscious." It's not just a coincidence when you meet someone on the street and they tell you their name is Som, but then later find out that your friend Som was just thinking about meeting up with you today.

That would be synchronicity! In 1902 he published The Psychology of Dementia Praecox (later translated into English as Schizophrenia), which laid out his theory about how mental illnesses develop over time based on their symptoms rather than just treating them as diseases like other doctors did at this time period (There was more going on inside someone's head than just chemicals)

This concept was first introduced by Carl Gustav Jung in 1952 and has since been further developed by other thinkers, including Wolfgang Pauli and Arthur Koestler. These coincidences seem to be more than just random chance occurrences, and they often occur when we contemplate our deepest desires and motivations.

This idea may sound strange at first glance; however, many people have experienced something similar themselves: they were thinking about someone they hadn't seen in a while only to run into them unexpectedly later on, or perhaps while driving home from work one day it suddenly started raining heavily outside even though there wasn't any rain forecasted for that evening...these types of events happen all around us every single day!

His contribution to the concept is significant because it allows us to understand how an individual's inner life can be reflected in external events without any apparent cause-and-effect relationship between them. Jungian psychology suggests that our minds may be able to influence objects in ways other than through ordinary cause-and-effect relationships; this phenomenon has been called psychokinesis (PK).

> "*There is no rule that is true under all circumstances, for this is the real and not a statistical world. Because the statistical method shows only the average aspects, it creates an artificial and predominantly conceptual picture of reality.*
> *— Carl Jung*"

Every Single Moment Unfolds For A Reason

The unconscious mind acts as an intermediary between our conscious thoughts and reality. This ability comes from our psychic energy being able to access parts of ourselves outside of our immediate awareness—those parts which may be hidden from view due to fear or shame (e.g., "I'm afraid people won't like me if they know what I really think").

> "*Do not cling to the shore, but set sail for exotic lands and places no longer found on maps. Walk on hallowed grounds. Blaze new trails. The term synchronicity was coined in the 1950s by the Swiss psychologist Carl Jung, to describe uncanny coincidences that seem to be meaningful. The Greek roots are syn-, "together," and khronos, "time." Synchronicity is the effector of Gnosis. Explore the Bogomils and the Cathars not just through books but, if at all possible, by visiting their lands, cemeteries and descendants. Finally, explore the most contemporary manifestations of Gnosticism: the writings of C.G. Jung, Jorge Luis Borges, Aleister Crowley, René Guénon, Hermann Hesse, Philip K. Dick, and Albert Camus. Gradually, you will begin to understand the various thought currents and systems existing in Gnosticism, and you will have begun to understand what does and does not appeal to you in Gnostic thought.*
> *— Laurence Galian, Alien Parasites: 40 Gnostic Truths to Defeat the Archon Invasion!*"

The idea is based on two main concepts: archetypes and the collective unconscious. The first concept refers to universal symbols (like water representing emotions) that exist within our collective unconscious; these symbols can appear in dreams or visions as images or ideas without being directly experienced by us beforehand. The second concept refers to a part of our minds where all human beings share certain thoughts, feelings, memories, and experiences regardless of race or culture—this part is called "the collective unconscious."

The power of synchronicity comes from its ability to reveal things about yourself that you may not have been aware were there before; this can help you understand yourself better so that when similar situations arise again later down the road (and they will), you'll know how best handle them based on past experience with similar situations rather than reacting blindly based solely upon current circumstances alone which might make matters worse instead than better! But it can also be thought of as "divine intervention." Jung described synchronicity as an encounter between inner and outer reality, where you experience something unexplainable or out of the ordinary.

The premise is that every detail unfolds for a purpose; there are no coincidences—and if you're open to seeing them, they'll reveal themselves! The unconscious mind is not only a repository for repressed or forgotten experiences but also an active participant in our daily lives. They were too painful or traumatic (such as memories of childhood abuse), but also include any other information we are not currently aware of possessing—even if it's something as simple as knowing how to ride a bicycle without having been taught by someone else!

The unconscious influences our behavior and decision-making processes in ways we are often unaware of and unable to control. In other words, it's when you have an experience that feels like it has some sort of deeper meaning than what's obvious at face value—and this feeling can be triggered by anything from finding a penny on the ground (the first time) to seeing someone who looks exactly like your dead father (the second time).

The components of synchronicity include:

- **An experience**
- **A meaningful connection**
- **Timing**
- **Surprise**
- **A sense of awe**
- **Dreams**
- **Symbols**
- **Numbers**
- **"Random" events**
- **Conversations**
- **Spontaneous encounters**

The collective unconscious is a source of guidance and wisdom and synchronicities were a way of tapping into this collective wisdom. He saw synchronicities as a bridge between the conscious and unconscious mind and as a way of bringing about transformation and growth.

> "*The world stopped. All was silence but for their hearts trying to synchronize their crashing.*
> *— Helen Hoang, The Kiss Quotient*"

The psyche was not just limited to the individual but was connected to a larger, cosmic consciousness. Synchronicity occurs when an external event coincides with an inner state or feeling, and the resulting coincidence has a profound psychological effect.

The inner world refers to the individual's psyche, which consists of conscious and unconscious elements. The outer world refers to the physical world that we experience through our senses. These events could be internal, such as dreams or thoughts, or external, such as encounters with people or unexpected coincidences.

CHAPTER II

Jung's Impact On Psychology

Jung's impact on modern psychology is undeniable. Jung's work was also influenced by his interest in the mystical, the occult, and the supernatural. His theories have had an enormous effect on psychoanalytic theory, cognitive psychology, and psychotherapy.

Jung's ideas about the collective unconscious and archetypes have been especially influential in the development of post-Jungian approaches to dream analysis such as those of Marie-Louise von Franz and James Hillman. The concept of synchronicity has also been influential in fields such as quantum physics, where it was first described by Wolfgang Pauli as unus mundus (one world).

Jung's Concept Of Meaningfulness

One of the central concepts in Jung's theory is the idea of meaningfulness. He believed that humans have a natural inclination towards seeking meaning and purpose in their lives and that this search for meaning is an essential part of psychological growth and development.

The search for meaning is closely linked to the concept of individuation, It is the manner in which of becoming an all-encompassing and cohesive person. Individuation is the process of becoming aware of one's true self, and it involves integrating both the conscious and unconscious aspects of the psyche.

"Modern physics, having advanced into another world beyond conceivability, cannot dispense with the concept of a space-time continuum. Insofar as psychology penetrates into the unconscious, it probably has no alternative but to acknowledge the "indistinctness" or the impossibility of distinguishing between time and space, as well as their psychic relativity. The world of classical physics has not ceased to exist, and by the same token, the world of consciousness has not lost its validity against the unconscious... "Causality" is a psychologem (and originally a magic virtus) that formulates the connection between events and illustrates them as cause and effect. Another (incommensurable) approach that does the same thing in a different way is synchronicity. Both are identical in the higher sense of the term "connection" or "attachment." But on the empirical and practical level (i.e., in the real world), they are incommensurable and antithetical, like space and time.

[...]

I would now like to propose that instead of "causality" we have "(relatively) constant connection through effect," and instead of synchronicity we have (relatively) constant connection through contingency, equivalence, or "meaning.

— Carl Jung"

He believed that the search for meaning is a universal human experience and that it is not limited to any particular culture or society. And meaningfulness can be found in a wide variety of experiences, including art, religion, mythology, and personal relationships.

Jung believed that the search for meaning involves exploring the archetypes that are present in the psyche. He believed that individuals who are able to recognize and integrate their archetypes are better able to find meaning in their lives.

Jung's Concept Of Individuation

Jung's concept of the self is a key component in his theory of psychology. In Jungian thought, the self is essentially a person's entire personality, including their conscious and unconscious mind. It represents an individual's wholeness and totality—what makes them who they are as opposed to anyone else.

Individuation is the process of becoming a unique individual, which requires separating from the collective unconscious and embracing one's own personal experiences, thoughts, and feelings. It is also related to spirituality because it involves coming into contact with our inner selves—the part of us that exists beyond time or space. Jung believed that humans are born with an "archaic heritage"—a set of universal symbols or archetypes stored in our collective unconscious (the part of our minds where we store experiences).

> *"New points of view are not, as a rule, discovered in territory that is already known, but in out-of-the way places that may even be avoided because of their bad name. Carl Jung, Synchronicity: An Acausual Connecting Principle*
> *— Marc MacYoung"*

These archetypes help us make sense out of our lives by providing us with images and ideas about ourselves as well as others around us; however, when we ignore them they can cause problems such as anxiety or depression because they represent unfulfilled needs within ourselves that need attention before they become too strong for comfort.

The collective unconscious consists of all the inherited psychic structures that humans share due to our common evolutionary history as well as any experiences we have had before birth (e.g., during gestation). These include archetypes such as anima/animus (the feminine/masculine aspects within each person), shadow(s) (those parts of ourselves we reject or don't acknowledge), complexes (groups of related memories), etc.

> "*Synchronicity could be understood as an ordering system by means of which "similar" things coincide, without there being any apparent cause.*
> *— Carl Jung*"

Jung's Interpretations Of Dreams In Relation To Synchronicity

Jung believed that dreams could be a window into the deeper workings of the psyche and that they could reveal insights into a person's inner life. In dreams, seemingly unrelated images and events can be connected in a way that defies causal explanation.

For example, a dream about a snake might be connected to a real-life encounter with a snake, but it might also be related to other symbols and archetypes that are present in the dreamer's psyche.

Jung also believed that acausal orderedness could manifest in the form of archetypes. Archetypes are symbols that have a deep meaning and resonance for people across cultures and time periods.

> "*Jung never tired of saying this. After the past is explored, additional inquiry into yesterday does not lead to further healing. A change of attitude into the present does, and this change of attitude is exactly the business of a synchronicity.*
> *— Gary Bobroff, Knowledge In A Nutshell Carl Jung*"

Examples of archetypes include the mother, the hero, and the trickster. Archetypes are evidence of the deeper, underlying order in the universe, and they can be used to understand the meaning behind seemingly unrelated events. For example, you might be thinking about a particular topic or person, and then suddenly encounter that topic or person in multiple places throughout the day.

CHAPTER III

Jung's Concept Related To Synchronicity

Archetypes

In his book, The Archetypes and the Collective Unconscious, Jung defined an archetype as a "primordial image" that exists in the collective unconscious. Archetypes are universal images found across cultures through time; they appear in myths across many different cultures around the world (e.g., hero stories). These images are inherited from our ancestors and represent universal experiences or patterns of behavior.

Jung also believed that archetypes have a direct relationship with spirituality and synchronicity because they act as a bridge between the conscious mind (which he called the ego) and the collective unconscious (or soul). This means that when you have an experience of spirituality or synchronicity, it's because your ego has been opened up enough for you to access this deeper part of yourself through an archetype.

The archetype itself isn't fixed but rather flexible enough so that it can fit into different contexts without losing its meaning or significance over time; this means that although there may be differences between how different cultures express certain archetypes like motherhood or warlike behavior between nations today compared with those from ancient times due largely because technology has changed dramatically since then—nevertheless these same core ideas remain consistent throughout history despite how much societies might change over time due largely because human nature hasn't changed much either despite technological advancements being made constantly over centuries past present future generations living today might not realize just yet.

These archetypal images have an impact on how we perceive reality through dreams and fantasies as well as through artworks like paintings or sculptures.

The Shadow

Jung's concept of the shadow is a part of our psyche that contains all our repressed emotions, thoughts, and desires. It's often considered to be negative, but it can also include positive aspects that we have rejected or ignored. The shadow is connected to our collective unconscious—the shared experiences and ideas that we all have as humans.

The shadow represents everything you do not want to acknowledge about yourself because it makes you feel ashamed or uncomfortable; however, when you are able to accept your own darkness without judgment, then it becomes easier for others around us who may not be able to face their own shadows as well as we do at first glance (or ever).

> "*Only when it comes to explaining psychic phenomena of a minimal degree of clarity are we driven to assume that archetypes must have a nonpsychic aspect. Grounds for such a conclusion are supplied by the phenomena of synchronicity, which are associated with the activity of*

unconscious operators and have hitherto been regarded, or repudiated, as 'telepathy' etc. Scepticism should, however, be levelled only at incorrect theories and not at facts which exist in their own right. No unbiased observer can deny them. Resistance to the recognition of such facts rests principally on the repugnance people feel for an allegedly supernatural faculty tacked on to the psyche, like 'clairvoyance'. The very diverse and confusing aspects of these phenomena are, so far as I can see at present, completely explicable on the assumption of psychically relative space-time continuum. As soon as the psychic content crosses the threshold of consciousness, the synchronistic marginal phenomena disappear, time and space resume their accustomed sway, and consciousness is once more isolated in its subjectivity. We have here one of those instances which can best be understood in terms of the physicist's idea of 'complementarity'. When an unconscious content passes over into consciousness its synchronistic manifestation ceases; conversely, synchronistic phenomena can be evoked by putting the subject into an unconscious state (trance).
— Carl Jung, On the Nature of the Psyche"

The Anima And Animus

The anima and animus are archetypes that represent the feminine and masculine aspects of our personalities. They are part of the collective unconscious, which means they exist in all people—not just men or women.

The concept was developed by Carl Jung, who believed that these archetypes can be found in dreams and fantasies as well as myths from different cultures around the world. These archetypes were important because they help us understand ourselves better by showing us how we relate to others (i.e., how we view ourselves).

For example, if someone has an image of a strong woman who is powerful but also kind and nurturing in their dreams or fantasies then it might mean that person wants more balance between their masculine/feminine qualities; this would be an example of using your own personal experiences with these types of images as guidance on how best understand yourself better so you can achieve greater spiritual growth overall!

> "*That's the kind of question that got Carl Jung thinking about synchronicity (universal resonance) which is a little bit like Sheldrake's morphogenetic field and also, coincidentally, a little bit like the non-local effect in quantum mechanics.*
> *— Robert Anton Wilson, The New Inquisition: Irrational Rationalism and the Citadel of Science*"

Synchronicity And Meaningful Coincidences

Coincidences may be playful or serious in nature; they may be subtle or dramatic; they occur frequently or rarely—and yet all coincidences have one thing in common: they seem odd when we notice them because we do not expect them (or cannot explain them).

Coincidences happen every day; some people even consider themselves lucky because they experience more than their fair share! However, synchronicity is often confused with coincidence. A coincidence is when two or more events occur simultaneously without any apparent causal relationship.

For example, a person may be thinking of an old friend they haven't spoken to in years, and then they receive a phone call from that friend the same day. This could be considered a coincidence.

However, if the phone call was not just a friendly catch-up but instead, the friend offered the person a job opportunity that they had been seeking for years, then this would be considered a meaningful coincidence or synchronicity. In other words, synchronicity involves a connection between events that goes beyond mere chance.

> "*We put thirty spokes together and call it a wheel; But it is on the space where there is nothing that the utility of the wheel depends. We turn clay to make a vessel; But it is on the space where there is nothing that the utility of the vessel depends. We pierce doors and windows to make a house; And it is on these spaces where there is nothing that the utility of the house depends. Therefore just as we take advantage of what is, we should recognize the utility of what is not. [Ch. XL]*
> *— C.G. Jung, Synchronicity: An Acausal Connecting Principle*"

Collective Unconscious

The concept of collective unconscious was first introduced by Carl Jung in his book The Structure of the Psyche. The collective unconscious is an inherited set of human experiences, emotions, and ways of thinking. It contains archetypes—primordial images and concepts that we all share in common.

The idea behind this concept is that our minds are not simply blank slates at birth but rather have been shaped by our ancestors' experiences over thousands of years. For example, everyone has heard stories about "the hero" or "the princess" since they were young: these are examples of archetypes that exist within us all as part of our collective unconscious.

When we see someone doing something bravely or selflessly (like rescuing someone), we instinctively respond with admiration because there's something familiar about it—it reminds us of how someone else might act if they were put into similar circumstances; it triggers feelings from deep within ourselves because those feelings have been passed down through generations before us; they're part of who we are as human beings!

Jung believed that these connections between seemingly unrelated events occur due to their existence within our collective unconsciousness; therefore if one person experiences something related specifically to their own personal experiences then others who share similar traits will likely encounter similar situations too even though those events might not have happened yet!

The power of the unconscious to shape our lives is undeniable. Jung believed that our unconscious minds are constantly working on problems and coming up with solutions even when we're not aware of them. When something happens in your life that seems like it was meant for you—like getting a job offer from your favorite company or meeting someone who shares your interests—it may be because some part of your mind has been working on those issues without telling you about it until now!

It's also where we store memories from childhood, which can be accessed through dreams or flashbacks. Because it contains these memories and experiences, it has an enormous amount of information about how you see yourself, other people, and the world around you—and this information can affect how you interpret coincidences as meaningful or not.

These archetypes have been passed down through generations and can be found in every culture, whether they're aware of them or not. Synchronicity helps us understand how our actions affect others far beyond what we might expect or even realize; it's like being able to see inside someone else's mind by observing their behavior or surroundings (and vice versa).

Synchronicities can also act as messages from ourselves or other people who may be struggling with something important in their lives—they're signs from within ourselves about what needs attention so that we can make better choices going forward!

The more you understand how it works, the better you'll be able to use it to create meaningful coincidences. Connecting with your unconscious mind is key to recognizing synchronicities and understanding their significance.

CHAPTER IV

Causality Vs Synchronicity

Let's consider some common questions about life: Why are we here? What is my purpose? How do I find happiness and fulfillment? These are all important questions that everyone asks themselves at some point in their lives—and if you're reading this article right now then there's a good chance you're asking yourself these exact same questions! Let's take a look at how Carl Jung would answer these questions using his theory of synchronicity as our guide:

Why am I here on Earth? Because there must be some reason why everything happens exactly when it does instead of another time or place; therefore there must be some sort of order behind all things which makes them happen according to certain rules instead of just randomly stumbling into existence without any rhyme or reason whatsoever (which would be pretty scary).

> "*Naturally, every age thinks that all ages before it were prejudiced, and today we think this more than ever and are just as wrong as all previous ages that thought so. How often have we not seen the truth condemned! It is sad but unfortunately true that man learns nothing from history.*
> *— Carl Jung, Synchronicity: An Acausal Connecting Principle*"

What is my purpose in life? To find out what those rules are so that they can become clearer over time until eventually becoming clear enough where even someone who wasn't paying attention before could see them clearly now—which means anyone who wants answers should keep searching until finding something useful because once again...scary!

Causality Vs Synchronicity

In traditional scientific thinking, causality is the principle that every event has a cause and that these causes can be understood through empirical observation and experimentation.

For example, if a person gets sick after eating a particular food, we can identify the cause of their illness as the food they ate. Another example is, If you drop a glass on the floor and it breaks, then your dropping the glass was the cause of its breaking.

However, Jung believed that causality alone could not explain all of the events that we experience in our lives. He recognized that there are many events that seem to occur without any clear cause-and-effect relationship. To illustrate this concept, let's consider a hypothetical example. Imagine that a person is feeling anxious and uncertain about their career path. They have been considering quitting their job and pursuing a different line of work, but they are unsure if this is the right decision.

One day, while walking, they come across a book lying on the ground. They pick it up and notice that it is a biography of someone who made a major career change later in life and found great success. This coincidence might seem insignificant on its own, but to the person experiencing it, it could be a powerful synchronicity that provides the guidance and encouragement they need to pursue their own career change.

He also believed that synchronicities were more likely to occur during times of crisis or change when we are most open to new experiences and ideas. Another example is if someone has a dream about their deceased grandfather while they're sleeping next to their grandmother who happens to be wearing his favorite shirt that day. Carl Jung believed that causality was too limiting and failed to account for all occurrences in life; instead, he thought that synchronicity could explain these occurrences better than causality could.

Acausal Connection

Acausal connection refers to a type of connection that is not based on cause and effect. In other words, acausal connections are connections that occur without any apparent cause. Jung believed that acausal connections are an essential part of human experience and that they are closely linked to the concept of synchronicity.

Jung believed that synchronicity occurs when the individual is in a state of heightened awareness and that it is a manifestation of the unconscious. He believed that synchronicity is a way of accessing the collective unconscious, which is the repository of all human experience and knowledge. Jung believed that acausal connections are not limited to individual experiences, but can also occur on a collective level.

> "*We must remember that the rationalistic attitude of the West is not the only possible one and is not all-embracing, but is in many ways a prejudice and a bias that ought perhaps to be corrected.*"

Meaningfulness and Acausal Connections

He argues that we are all connected in some way and that this connection is expressed through symbols that appear in our dreams or waking life. Jung also believed that meaningful coincidences were caused by the unconscious mind of the person experiencing them.

He also argued that there was some kind of link between two seemingly unrelated things—like two people having similar thoughts at different times or finding something important after losing it—that could not be explained by science or logic alone but rather required an understanding of how meaning works within ourselves as well as our relationships with others.

The Concept Of Acausal Orderedness

He was also interested in the concept of acausal orderedness, which he believed was a fundamental principle in the universe. Jung's concept of acausal orderedness is based on his belief that the universe is governed by a fundamental principle of order, which is not based on cause and effect. Jung believed that these events, which appear to be random, are actually part of a larger pattern that is determined by this underlying order.

Jung also believed that this underlying order was connected to the concept of the unus mundus, which is the idea that all of reality is part of a single, unified whole. He believed that this unified whole was the source of the meaningful coincidences that occur in our lives and that these coincidences were evidence of the underlying order of the universe. To illustrate this concept, we can look at a real-life example. For instance, consider a situation in which a person is struggling with a difficult decision and is feeling overwhelmed.

Suddenly, they hear a song on the radio that contains lyrics that seem to perfectly describe their situation. This could be seen as an example of synchronicity, as it appears to be a meaningful coincidence that is connected to the person's internal psychological state. This could be seen as evidence of the underlying order of the universe, as it appears to be a meaningful coincidence that is connected to the person's internal psychological state. Another example of synchronicity can be seen in the concept of déjà vu. This is the feeling of having experienced a situation before, even though it is actually new to the person.

> "*Every emotional state produces an alteration of consciousness which Janet called abaissement du niveau mental; that is to say there is a certain narrowing of consciousness and a corresponding strengthening of the unconscious which, particularly in the case-of strong affects, is noticeable even to the layman.*
> *— C.G. Jung, Synchronicity*"

How To Recognize Synchronicity?

- **Recognize patterns:** The first step in recognizing synchronicity is to become aware of the patterns in your life. When you start paying attention, you may be surprised by how many coincidences there are around us all the time!

- **Understand the signs:** Once you've identified a pattern, ask yourself what it means or why it has occurred. This will help you determine if this is indeed a coincidence or something more meaningful than that—like a sign from your unconscious mind (or whatever else).
- **Be open to possibilities:** If there's something going on inside of yourself that feels significant enough for someone else's actions or words to trigger it—whether consciously or unconsciously—then chances are good that there's something deeper going on here than just chance alone would allow for!

CHAPTER V

In Our Deepest Desires And Motivations

Our deepest desires and motivations are the things that drive us in life. They are the things that guide our daily actions and decisions. However, synchronicity is connected to our deepest desires and motivations in several ways. Therefore, synchronicity can help us manifest our goals at a higher and spiritual level, as well as provide guidance along the way. Synchronicity often occurs when we are contemplating our deepest desires and motivations. For example, if you are thinking about a career change and then you meet someone who is doing the job you have always wanted to do, that is synchronicity.

This kind of synchronicity can be a sign that you are on the right path and that you should pursue your desires and motivations. But sometimes we are not aware of what we truly want or what is driving us. Synchronicity can bring these things to the surface and help us to see them more clearly. The power of the psyche is something we all experience on a daily basis but may not fully understand or appreciate. Therefore, synchronicity can be a sign that we are in this state of alignment and that our desires and motivations are starting to manifest in our lives.

For example, if you keep running into people who are involved in environmental activism, that might be a sign that you have a deep desire to make a positive impact on the environment. Therefore, when we are in alignment with our desires and motivations and aware of synchronicity, we are more likely to attract the people, resources, and opportunities we need to achieve our goals.

Synchronicity and The Power Of Gratitude

It's easy to see how gratitude can help us manifest our desires, but what about synchronicity? How does it fit in? The answer lies in the fact that gratitude is a powerful emotion that creates positive energy and attracts more good things into your life.

When you're grateful for what you have, you're sending out signals that say "I'm happy with my life as it is now." This sends out ripples of energy into the universe which attracts more things like them into your experience—whether those things are people or situations or opportunities for growth and learning.

If you want more meaningful coincidences in your life—and we all do!—then cultivate gratitude by being thankful for what is already there rather than focusing on what could be or should be different from where things currently stand (e.g., "I wish I had more money" vs., "I am grateful for what little money I do have").

The secret is when you're grateful for something, it's easier to notice coincidences that happen around that thing. For example, if someone is grateful for their job and they see a sign saying "work" while driving down the road, they will notice it more than someone who isn't grateful for their job would have.

Synchronicity In Experiences

If synchronicity has been working in your favor lately—and I hope it has!—then congratulations! But don't forget about those times when things didn't go as planned (or even worse: when they went horribly wrong).

In those instances too we should consider whether there was any hidden meaning behind our experiences; perhaps through them, we learned valuable lessons about ourselves or others around us which would otherwise have remained unknown until much later on down life's road...

Synchronicity can also be explored in the experiences we create for ourselves. The concept of serendipity, or "the faculty of making happy and unexpected discoveries by accident," is an important one to understand when exploring synchronicity in daily life.

Serendipitous moments are often thought of as lucky or accidental occurrences, but they can also be seen as opportunities to be seized upon and used as stepping stones toward creating a more meaningful future experience.

The idea that everything happens for a reason is not new; however, it's rarely discussed in terms of everyday life experiences—especially those that may seem insignificant at first glance (like finding money on the ground).

> "*One consistent experience in all these experiments is the fact that the number of hits scored tends to sink after the first attempt, and the results then become negative. But if, for some inner or outer reason, there is a freshening of interest on the subject's part, the score rises again. Lack of interest and boredom are negative factors; enthusiasm, positive expectation, hope, and belief in the possibility of ESP make for good results and seem to be the real conditions which determine whether there are going to be any results at all.*
> *— C.G. Jung, Synchronicity*"

When we begin looking at our lives through this lens, we begin seeing how all things have a purpose: even if there isn't always an obvious connection between cause and effect immediately apparent from our perspective now—or ever—it doesn't mean there isn't one there somewhere!

Synchronicity In Everyday Life

Synchronicity is a phenomenon that can be observed in everyday life. Here are some examples of synchronicities that might occur in everyday life:

- You're thinking about someone you haven't seen in years, then they call or email out of the blue.
- Your favorite song comes on while driving down the street where your ex-boyfriend lives (or used to live).
- You hear an advertisement on TV advertising something that was recently purchased by someone close to you—and they didn't tell anyone else about their purchase!
- If you're looking for a job and keep getting interviews but no offers, it might be because your subconscious mind knows something is wrong with the job prospect. You may need to look closer at what's really going on before accepting such an offer. Or maybe there's another opportunity coming up that will suit your needs better than this one does!
- You're looking for a new job and you find one that looks promising. You apply, but the company tells you they can't hire anyone at this time. A week later, they call back and say they have an opening after all and would like to interview you again.

- Your friend mentions that she has been trying to contact another friend who lives far away but hasn't heard from her in weeks—and then right after this conversation ends with your friend, your phone rings with an unknown number on caller ID (which is actually your long-lost friend). You answer without thinking twice about it because it seems so unlikely that she would call now after so long without contact; however, when asked if she could speak with "so-and-so" (the name of your mutual acquaintance), there's silence on the other end before she says yes!
- You were driving to work one morning when you saw a bumper sticker on the rear of someone else's roadster that said "Love is the Answer." You had been thinking about this very topic for several days, so it was quite meaningful for you to see this message in such an unexpected place.
- A few years ago you started dating someone who lived across town from you and worked at night (You work during the day). It happened that your schedules aligned perfectly so that you could spend time together after work every day for about six months before she moved away for work reasons (and you broke up). You didn't realize how lucky you were until later—it seemed like fate!
- You notice an advertisement for something that piques your attention or excites you while watching television or surfing online; later in conversation with someone else who shares similar interests, he mentions having seen exactly the same ad recently too (and even had similar thoughts about buying whatever product was being advertised). This could be interpreted as evidence that there exists some sort of connection between these

two people—a possible reason why this particular advertisement would appeal equally strongly both times around!

- You buy a new car and then see that same model on the street within days of buying it (or vice versa).
- You have a dream about something that later comes true in real life—for example, dreaming about winning an award, the lottery, or getting married before either event actually happens in real life.
- You meet someone who has just moved into your neighborhood and they invite you over for coffee. Afterward, they mention that their son is looking for a tutor for math and science—and it turns out that this person went to school with one of your friends!
- Your roommate has been complaining about how expensive groceries are lately; so when she leaves town on business for a few days, she puts some money in an envelope with instructions for how much should go toward food each week (and reminds herself not to buy anything else). When she returns home from her trip, there's no shortage of delicious snacks waiting for her—but what really gets her excited is finding out why: Her boyfriend had cooked up all sorts of treats while she was gone!
- A woman buys tickets online before heading off on vacation, but when she goes back later in order not only to see whether any seats become available but also purchase them if necessary...she finds herself sitting next door to someone who works at Google!

CHAPTER VI

Examples of Synchronicity

Carl Jung's Red Book

One of Jung's most famous works is The Red Book, a collection of his own dreams, fantasies, and reflections. The Red Book was a deeply personal work, and Jung never intended it to be published during his lifetime.

Carl Jung was struggling with his own unconscious and was feeling lost and confused. One day, he had a dream in which he was in a library and discovered a book bound in red leather. In the dream, he felt a strong urge to read the book but didn't have time.

A few days later, Jung went to visit a patient who was experiencing similar feelings of confusion and despair. The patient showed him a drawing that he had made of a book that he had dreamed about. It was bound in red leather, just like the book in Jung's dream. The patient had never met Jung before and had no knowledge of his dream.

This experience of synchronicity inspired Jung to explore the concept further and led to the development of his theory of the collective unconscious.

However, after his death, the book was discovered and published, providing an insight into Jung's inner world. One of the most striking features of The Red Book is the synchronicities that Jung describes.

In the early 1900s, Jung began experiencing vivid dreams and visions that he felt were connected to the collective unconscious. He began to record these experiences in a journal, which he called "The Red Book".

Over the next several years, Jung continued to work on his journal, adding drawings and paintings to his entries. He felt that the images he was creating were symbolic of his inner process and were a way of tapping into the collective wisdom of the unconscious.

In 1913, Jung had a dream in which he saw a flood covering Europe. He felt that this dream was a warning of the coming of World War I. He also felt that he needed to complete his Red Book before the war began.

Jung worked feverishly on his book, and by 1914, he had completed it. The book was a symbolic representation of his inner journey and was filled with images and symbols that were meaningful to him. He felt that the completion of the book was a significant event in his life and that it had been guided by a larger, universal force.

Carl Jung's Dream About Egyptian Jewelry

Jung had a dream in which he was given a piece of Egyptian jewelry. He received an unexpected gift on a subsequent day from a client who had lately returned from Egypt.

The gift was a piece of jewelry that was almost identical to the one he had seen in his dream. This event convinced Jung that there was a meaningful connection between his dream and the gift he received.

The Life Of Vincent Van Gogh

Vincent van Gogh was a Dutch post-impressionist painter who is widely regarded as one of the world's finest painters. He had a turbulent life, marked by poverty, mental illness, and a difficult relationship with his family. He struggled to find his place in the world and to make sense of his own existence.

Despite these challenges, he was deeply spiritual and found solace in nature, which he saw as a reflection of the divine. He was also deeply interested in religion and read extensively about Christian theology. His paintings often have a spiritual quality, with vibrant colors and bold brushstrokes that evoke a sense of awe and wonder.

His life and work illustrate many of Jung's ideas about spirituality. His struggles with mental illness can be seen as a manifestation of his attempt to integrate his conscious and unconscious aspects. His artistic expression was a form of spiritual practice, allowing him to connect with the transcendent and to express his innermost thoughts and feelings.

> "*Natural laws are statistical truths, which means that they are completely valid only when we are dealing with macrophysical quantities. In the realm of very small quantities prediction becomes uncertain, if not impossible, because very small quantities no longer behave in accordance with the known natural laws.*
> *— C.G. Jung, Synchronicity*"

As a result, Van Gogh's paintings keep on moving and impact people all around the world, demonstrating the ability of devotion to go beyond time and location.

The Butterflies

In the mid-1990s, a group of scientists were studying the migration patterns of monarch butterflies. They had tagged and released several butterflies in their lab in Canada and were tracking their movements using radio telemetry.

One day, one of the scientists received a call from a friend in Mexico. The friend reported that he had found a tagged butterfly in his garden, which had traveled more than 2,000 miles from Canada.

This was an incredible feat for a butterfly, but what made this even more remarkable was that the scientist had just been discussing the possibility of monarch butterflies migrating to Mexico.

The synchronicity of the conversation and the discovery of the tagged butterfly seemed to suggest a deeper connection between the two events.

The Birth Of A Son

A man and his wife had been trying to have a child for years but were unsuccessful. They had tried every medical intervention available, but nothing seemed to work.

One day, the man had a dream in which he was walking through a garden and found a sapling that he took home and planted in his yard. In the dream, he knew that this was his son.

A few months later, the man's wife became pregnant, and they had a healthy baby boy. When they returned home from the hospital, they discovered that a sapling had grown overnight in their yard. The sapling was exactly like the one the man had seen in his dream.

The synchronicity of the dream and the birth of their son seemed to suggest a deeper connection between the two events.

The Writer And The Owl

A writer was struggling to find inspiration for a new book. She had been searching for a topic that would really capture her imagination and spark her creativity.

One night, she was sitting outside on her porch, feeling discouraged and uninspired, when an owl flew down and landed on the railing right in front of her.

The writer had always loved owls, but she had never seen one up close like this. She felt a deep sense of connection to the owl and was struck by its beauty and grace.

Over the next few days, the writer started to see owls everywhere she went. She saw them in pictures, on TV, and even in real life. She started to feel like the owls were trying to tell her something.

Eventually, she realized that her deep desire was to write a book about owls. She had always loved them, but she had never considered writing a book about them before.

The synchronicity of seeing owls everywhere was a sign that this was her true passion and that she should pursue it.

Woman's Struggle For The Job

One example of synchronicity is the story of a woman who had been struggling with a difficult decision regarding her career. She had been feeling stuck and uncertain about what path to take when one day she received an unexpected call from a former colleague.

The colleague told her that they had just started a new job and that they were looking for someone to join their team. The woman realized that this job would be a perfect fit for her, and decided to take the opportunity. She later reflected on how the call had come at just the right time and felt that it was a sign that she was on the right path.

Old Man's Quest For His Health Issues

Another example of synchronicity is the story of an old man who was struggling with a health issue. He had been seeing a doctor for months but had not been able to find a solution to his problem. He stumbled upon a book one day while shopping in a bookshop about a natural remedy that he had never heard of before.

He decided to give it a try and found that it worked wonders for his condition. He later reflected on how the book had appeared at just the right time and felt that it was a sign that he was meant to find this solution.

Finding A Job

For example, if you're looking for a new job and decide to apply at your favorite restaurant because it has an opening, but then find out that your best friend works there, this would be considered synchronicity because it brings together two different worlds: yours and theirs (the restaurant).

This can also happen with people; if you meet someone who shares many interests with you or has similar personality traits as yours, this is also considered synchronicity because they are bringing together two different things—their selves and yours—to create something new and valuable for both parties involved in this union.

Reminder

One example of synchronicity is when someone sees something on TV or hears about something in their everyday life that reminds them of another person without either party being aware beforehand (e.g., seeing someone wearing the same shirt).

Quantum Entanglement In Relationship

Another example would be having two people think about each other at exactly the same moment without knowing why; maybe one person was thinking about calling but didn't want to bother anyone else.

In either case, these events happen all around us every day; we just need some practice noticing them so we can start using them more intentionally too!

For example: imagine you've been feeling anxious about something for weeks, but when it finally happens (whatever "it" may be), you find yourself calm and relaxed instead of stressed out or panicked as usual.

> "*Synchronistic phenomena prove the simultaneous occurrence of meaningful equivalences in heterogeneous, causally unrelated processes; in other words, they prove that a content perceived by an observer can, at the same time, be represented by an outside event, without any causal connection. From this it follows either that the psyche cannot be localized in space, or that space is relative to the psyche. The same applies to the temporal determination of the psyche and the psychic relativity of time. I do not need to emphasize that the verification of these findings must have far-reaching consequences.*"

This could be considered a coincidence because there's no obvious reason why this particular thing would make you feel better; however, if we look deeper into how each person experiences the world around them through their own lens of meaning and belief systems then we can see how this might actually make sense within their personal experience!

Thinking of Someone

Imagine you're thinking about taking up painting again after years away from it; then one day you see an advertisement for an art class on TV—and this happens just when your mind was occupied with thoughts about painting!

If you were thinking about your friend while they called you on their birthday or if you saw an ad for something while browsing Facebook and then later bought it online (without having planned on doing so).

Synchronicities can be small moments that make us stop in our tracks and think about how amazing life is or they can be larger events like winning the lottery when all odds were against us or getting into college after being rejected by every other school we applied to!

> "*The most that can fairly be demanded is that the number of individual observations shall be as high as possible. If this number, statistically considered, falls within the limits of chance expectation, then it has been statistically proved that it was a question of chance; but no explanation has thereby been furnished. There has merely been an exception to the rule.*"

The phone call and your thoughts about your friend were not causally related—there was no physical connection between the two events. These events are not merely coincidental but have meaning beyond what we can perceive with our five senses.

However, they were connected through their underlying meaning, in this case, the connection you share with your friend.

Dreaming About Someone Close To You

If you dream about someone you haven't seen in years and then run into them at the grocery store later that day—that would be considered synchronicity because there's no obvious reason (it wasn't planned) why this would happen (like they live near you).

This means that something happens outside our perception of reality; it doesn't follow any rules we know about yet still exists as part of our universe!

CHAPTER VII

In The Power Of Intuition

Intuition is defined as "the ability to understand something immediately, without the need for conscious reasoning." It's often referred to as "gut feeling" or "women's intuition," but it's actually a very real phenomenon that we all experience every day—even if we don't recognize it as such at first glance! In fact, many people find themselves experiencing more synchronicities than usual when they're going through difficult times or transitions in their lives (such as moving house).

This may seem like an odd coincidence at first glance—after all, why would there be more coincidences happening around me now than ever before? But if we look deeper into what this means from an intuitive perspective. Therefore, synchronicity and intuition are closely related concepts. In both cases, there seems to be some kind of psychic connection between two people or events—but how does this happen? The more we trust our inner voice (or gut feeling), the better we'll be able to recognize these meaningful coincidences when they occur.

The more you develop your intuition, the more likely you are to recognize synchronicity. One way to do this is by paying attention to your gut feelings about situations and people in your life. If something feels "off" or "wrong," there's probably a reason for it! Your intuition may be trying to tell you something important about what's happening right now—or what could happen in the future if things don't change.

Intuition is a powerful force that can be used to identify and create meaningful coincidences. Synchronicity and intuition are two sides of the same coin. In fact, synchronicity can help us recognize our own intuition by showing us what we need to pay attention to in order for our instincts to come through clearly.

> "*Rhine's experiments confront us with the fact that there are events which are related to one another experimentally, and in this case meaningfully, without there being any possibility of proving that this relation is a causal one, since the "transmission" exhibits none of the known properties of energy.*
> *— C.G. Jung, Synchronicity*"

For example: if someone asks me if I want coffee or tea at lunchtime, I'll usually say "coffee" because that's what my gut tells me—but sometimes my gut also tells me "tea," even though my conscious mind isn't sure why yet! In these cases (and many others), being open-minded enough about your choices will allow them both space within which they can grow into something bigger than either option alone could ever be on its own.

> "*There is an odd synchronicity in the way parallel lives veer to touch one another, change direction, and then come close again and again until they connect and hold for whatever it was that fate intended to happen.*
> *— Ann Rule*"

Therefore, it's important to recognize the role of intuition in synchronicity because it can help you notice when something special is happening. When you're trying to find meaning in your experiences and relationships, it's helpful to look back at the past few months or years of your life and see if there are any patterns or connections between them.

If there are no obvious connections between two events or people—or even three or four events/people—that doesn't mean that there isn't one! Therefore, intuition helps us recognize these patterns when they appear before our eyes (or minds).

CHAPTER VIII

In Quantum Mechanics

In the early 20th century, quantum mechanics was still in its infancy. Though it had been discovered that subatomic particles were inherently unpredictable and could behave as both waves and particles (a phenomenon known as wave-particle duality), scientists were still trying to figure out how this related to the macroscopic world we see around us every day. If you're a fan of quantum physics and the whole idea of parallel universes, then you might be interested in synchronicity. This is because the two are related: in fact, Jung believed that synchronistic events could help us understand quantum mechanics better.

In quantum physics (the study of subatomic particles), entanglement is a phenomenon where two particles become connected so that they share information even when separated by great distances from each other. For example, if you measure an electron on Earth and find out its position with respect to an atomic nucleus—let's say it's three feet away from the said nucleus—then that same electron would also have been three feet away from another atomic nucleus on Mars at exactly the same time as well if we measured there too!

This means that these two electrons are somehow "entangled" through space-time; they exist simultaneously throughout both locations even though neither one has traveled there yet (or perhaps ever will). This idea led Einstein to call entanglement "spooky action at a distance" because it violates our classical understanding of causality: one event happening after another due to some sort of connection between them through time or space rather than simply existing together simultaneously without any apparent reason why they should behave this way together instead of separately.

Carl Jung hoped that he could use his understanding of synchronicity to explain some of these phenomena in a way that would make sense scientifically—and he did just that! In 1952, he published an article titled "Synchronicity: An Acausal Connecting Principle" which explored how quantum entanglement might be related to synchronicity. Firstly, Synchronicity suggests that events are linked based on their meaning rather than their cause-and-effect relationships. In quantum mechanics, particles are known to interact with each other in non-local ways that go beyond traditional notions of causality.

At first glance, it may seem like there is little overlap between Synchronicity and Quantum Mechanics. However, upon closer examination of both theories, there are several connections that can be made.

For example, two entangled particles separated by vast distances will instantly affect each other's properties when one is observed or measured. These entangled particles seem to communicate information instantaneously across space and time—something that was previously thought impossible according to classical physics.

While this may seem like science fiction or fantasy, it has been empirically verified through experimentation numerous times over the last century. This odd phenomenon could suggest an underlying interconnectedness between all things in the universe—much like how Synchronicity implies everything is connected through meaningful coincidences.

However, In mainstream science, everything happens for a reason—if A causes B then it should always happen in the same way under the same conditions. But Quantum Mechanics shows us that things aren't always so clear-cut or predictable. Particles can exist in multiple states until they are observed, leading some scientists to argue that observation itself creates reality.

> "*I do believe in an everyday sort of magic -- the inexplicable connectedness we sometimes experience with places, people, works of art and the like; the eerie appropriateness of moments of synchronicity; the whispered voice, the hidden presence, when we think we're alone.*
> *— Charles de Lint*"

Similarly, Synchronicity suggests that they may be connected through their spiritual or symbolic significance. This idea challenges traditional scientific methods that rely solely on empirical observation and measurable evidence. However, some researchers have suggested that synchronicity may be explained by the principles of quantum mechanics. Here are some of the connections that have been proposed:

1. Non-locality: Quantum mechanics suggests that particles can be entangled, meaning that even though they exist apart by huge lengths of time, the state of one particle is reliant on the state of another. Similarly, synchronicity proposes that events that seem unrelated on the surface may be connected on a deeper level. Both theories suggest that there is a type of non-locality at work in the universe.

2. Observer effect: In quantum mechanics, the observer effect suggests that the act of observing a particle changes its state. Similarly, some researchers suggest that the act of observing synchronistic events may change their meaning or significance.

3. Probability: Quantum mechanics proposes that particles can exist in multiple states simultaneously and that the state that is observed is determined by probability. Similarly, synchronicity suggests that meaningful coincidences occur based on probability rather than cause and effect.

4. Connectedness: Quantum mechanics suggests that everything in the universe is connected and that the behavior of particles is dependent on the larger system in which they exist. Similarly, synchronicity proposes that events are connected on a deeper level and that everything in the universe is interconnected.

While these connections are intriguing, it's important to note that they are still speculative. There is no direct evidence to support the idea that synchronicity is linked to quantum mechanics, and some researchers are skeptical of the idea. Despite this, the connections between these two theories are fascinating and offer a new way of thinking about the universe. Whether or not they are ultimately proven to be linked, they both challenge our understanding of cause and effect and suggest that there may be deeper patterns and connections at work in the universe.

Finally, both Synchronicity and Quantum Mechanics suggest the presence of unseen forces operating in our universe. Jung believed in the existence of a collective unconscious—a shared repository of ancestral memories and experiences that transcends individual consciousness.

In a similar vein, quantum mechanics operates under the assumption that there exists a "quantum field"—an invisible force that permeates the entire universe and affects how particles interact with each other. In conclusion, while Carl Jung's theory of Synchronicity may seem unrelated to quantum mechanics at first glance, there are several fundamental connections between them.

> "*According to Vedanta, there are only two symptoms of enlightenment, just two indications that a transformation is taking place within you toward a higher consciousness. The first symptom is that you stop worrying. Things don't bother you anymore. You become light-hearted and full of joy. The second symptom is that you encounter more and more meaningful coincidences in your life, more and more synchronicities. And this accelerates to the point where you actually experience the miraculous. (quoted by Carol Lynn Pearson in Consider the Butterfly)*
> *— Deepak Chopra, Synchrodestiny: Harnessing the Infinite Power of Coincidence to Create Miracles*"

Both theories imply a deeper interconnectedness between all things in the universe and challenge our traditional understanding of cause-and-effect relationships. By exploring these connections further, we may gain new insights into the nature of reality and our place within it.

CHAPTER IX

In The Creative Process

Synchronicity, according to Jung, has a profound impact on our creative process because it helps us make sense of our experiences. Creative people often experience synchronicities as they encounter unconventional ideas and try to connect seemingly unrelated topics. They are more likely to notice patterns and connections that others might overlook. This ability makes them more receptive to insights from their unconscious mind.

Jung wrote extensively about the creative process in his book, "Psychology of the Unconscious." He believed that the creative process was a form of active imagination, where the individual would actively engage with the unconscious to bring forth new ideas and insights. According to Jung, the unconscious was a source of creativity that was often blocked by the conscious mind. Therefore, the creative process involved the integration of conscious and unconscious elements.

Jung believed that synchronicity played a crucial role in the integration of conscious and unconscious elements in the creative process. He argued that synchronistic events could help an individual to access the unconscious and bring forth new insights and ideas. For example, a synchronistic event might occur when an individual is struggling with a creative block. This event might be a chance encounter with a person who provides a new perspective or a seemingly random conversation that sparks a new idea.

He also believed that creativity was not solely the product of individual genius or inspiration, but rather emerged from a complex web of interrelated factors. Jung saw the creative process as a form of self-discovery, a way of tapping into the unconscious mind and accessing deeper levels of insight and meaning. This, in turn, could inspire them to create works of art or literature that resonated with others and helped to shape the cultural zeitgeist.

> "*Each man had only one genuine vocation - to find the way to himself....His task was to discover his own destiny - not an arbitrary one - and to live it out wholly and resolutely within himself. Everything else was only a would-be existence, an attempt at evasion, a flight back to the ideals of the masses, conformity and fear of one's own inwardness.*
> *— Herman Hesse*"

Jung's ideas about synchronicity and the creative process continue to influence thinkers and artists today. Many writers, musicians, and visual artists draw on Jung's insights as they seek to tap into the mysterious and elusive nature of creativity.

Synchronicity And The Inner Process

The inner process of the individual plays an important role in this phenomenon—the psyche can be seen as a filter through which all external events must pass before they become meaningful to us. For example, if you're feeling depressed and uninterested in anything outside yourself at the moment, then it's unlikely that any external event will seem synchronistic to you because they don't fit into your current state of mind.

This means that we must first look inside ourselves before looking outward for signs of synchronicity; only then will we be able to recognize them when they appear! The concept of "meaningful relationships" also plays an important role in Jungian theory; these relationships are said not only between people but also between objects or ideas (e.g., between dreams).

In order for something like this last example from above—a dream about an object—to count as being truly synchronistic rather than just coincidental coincidence requires some sort of connection between those two things: perhaps both dreamer and object share similar qualities such as being old fashioned?

> "*Life sometimes gets so bogged down in the details, you forget you are living it. There is always another appointment to be met, another bill to pay, another symptom presenting, another uneventful day to be notched onto the wooden wall. We have synchronized our watches, studied our calendars, existed in minutes, and completely forgotten to step back and see what we've accomplished.*
> *— Jodi Picoult, My Sister's Keeper*"

Or maybe both belong within certain groups (elderly people)? Whatever their connection might be here though doesn't matter so much right now since what matters most right now is simply understanding how these kinds of interactions work within ourselves first before moving on to bigger questions like "Why?"

CHAPTER X

In Our Relationships

Synchronicities can happen in relationships, too! When you're with someone who understands you on such a deep level that it seems like they know exactly what you need before even asking for it—that's synchronicity. Or maybe there was an instance where one of your friends said something so perfectly timed that it felt like fate had brought them into your life at just the right moment? That too would be considered synchronicity!

> "*I asked the universe for serendipity and you walked through my door.*
> *— Nikki Rowe*"

Therefore, synchronicity can also help us understand our relationships better by helping us identify what's really going on beneath surface-level interactions with others (and ourselves). We all know that relationships are complex and multifaceted, but synchronicity can play a significant role in shaping them. Synchronistic events can occur in relationships, highlighting the connection and meaning behind the interactions between two people.

For example, a couple might be having a discussion about a particular topic, and the television or radio might suddenly start playing a song that relates to the topic they are discussing. This event can act as a reminder or a confirmation of the connection that still exists between the couple. It can also provide an opportunity for them to explore the topic in more depth, leading to a deeper understanding of each other.

> “*You know those moments when everything is exactly the way it was meant to be? When you find yourself and your entire universe aligning in perfect synchronization, and you know you couldn’t possibly be more content? I was inside that very moment, and fully conscious of it.*
> *— Alice Clayton, Wallbanger*”

Another example of synchronicity in relationships can be seen in the timing of events. For instance, a couple might both have a sudden urge to take a walk at the same time, without either of them mentioning it to the other. As they walk, they might discover something new or unexpected, leading to a deeper connection between them. Such synchronistic events can create a sense of harmony and unity in the relationship.

Synchronicity can also be observed in the way people meet and form relationships. For example, two people might meet in a seemingly random way, only to discover later that they share a common interest or background. This coincidence can act as a catalyst for their relationship and provide a sense of destiny or purpose. In some cases, people might meet in seemingly random circumstances, only to discover that they have been linked by a series of events that occurred before they met. Such synchronistic events can provide a sense of awe and wonder and can lead to a deepening of the relationship.

> “*In this new year, may you have a deep understanding of your true value and worth, an absolute faith in your unlimited potential, peace of*

mind in the midst of uncertainty, the confidence to let go when you need to, acceptance to replace your resistance, gratitude to open your heart, the strength to meet your challenges, great love to replace your fear, forgiveness and compassion for those who offend you, clear sight to see your best and true path, hope to dispel obscurity, the conviction to make your dreams come true, meaningful and rewarding synchronicities, dear friends who truly know and love you, a childlike trust in the benevolence of the universe, the humility to remain teachable, the wisdom to fully embrace your life exactly as it is, the understanding that every soul has its own course to follow, the discernment to recognize your own unique inner voice of truth, and the courage to learn to be still.

— Janet Rebhan"

Synchronicity and Our Experiences

Experiences are another area where synchronicity can be observed. Synchronistic events can occur in a wide range of experiences, from everyday occurrences to life-changing events. For example, a person might be thinking about a particular problem, only to have a stranger come up to them and offer a solution. This event can be seen as a synchronistic event, providing a sense of connection and meaning in the person's life.

Another example of synchronicity in experiences can be seen in the way events seem to unfold in a person's life. For instance, a person might have a series of seemingly unrelated experiences that lead them to a particular realization or insight. These experiences might seem coincidental, but in hindsight, they can be seen as part of a larger plan or purpose. Such synchronistic events can provide a sense of meaning and purpose in a person's life.

Using Synchronicity For Self-Reflection

Synchronicity can be used to gain insight into our lives, but it's important to be mindful and attentive. You will need to pay attention to your environment and your thoughts in order for this technique to work. The potential for personal growth is enormous when you use synchronicity as a tool for self-reflection. By being aware of what's going on around you, you may find that there are things happening around us all the time that we can learn from if we just look closely enough!

> "*The great Sufi poet and philosopher Rumi once advised his students to write down the three things they most wanted in life. If any item on the list clashes with any other item, Rumi warned, you are destined for unhappiness. Better to live a life of single-pointed focus, he taught. But what about the benefits of living harmoniously among extremes? What if you could somehow create an expansive enough life that you could synchronize seemingly incongruous opposites into a worldview that excludes nothing?*
> *— Elizabeth Gilbert, Eat, Pray, Love*"

Tips To Use Synchronicity For Self-Reflection

1: Keep A Journal Of Your Synchronistic Events

This can involve recording any events or encounters that seem too coincidental to be mere chance and reflecting on their possible meanings. By doing this, individuals can begin to see patterns and connections that they may not have noticed before, and can gain a deeper understanding of the underlying forces at play in their lives.

2: Practice Mindfulness and Awareness

By paying attention to the present moment, and being open to unexpected experiences, individuals can become more attuned to the synchronistic events that occur in their lives. When you notice yourself feeling a certain way, ask yourself what the synchronistic event was that occurred just before the feeling arose. Then consider whether there might be some connection between these two events (perhaps even something deeper than mere coincidence).

> "*When you stop existing and you start truly living, each moment of the day comes alive with the wonder and synchronicity.*
> *— Steve Maraboli, Life, the Truth, and Being Free*"

This will help you become more aware of how your thoughts, feelings, and actions affect each other—and ultimately lead toward greater self-knowledge and understanding about who you really are!

3: Practice Meditation

Another way of increasing our ability to recognize synchronicity is through meditation, which has been shown by science (and countless personal experiences) as being an effective method for developing our sixth sense: telepathy between people with open minds who are willing participants in this process; also known as clairvoyance/ clairaudience etc.

CHAPTER XI

Under The Guidance From The Universal Want

The universe is a powerful force that can help you create meaningful coincidences in your life. The more you align with this force, the more synchronicities you'll encounter. Synchronistic events can also be observed in the way people receive messages, guidance, signs, and symbols from the universe or a higher power.

For example, a person might have a dream that provides them with a solution to a problem they have been struggling with. This dream might seem like a coincidence, but in reality, it can be seen as a synchronistic event, providing guidance and direction in the person's life.

For instance, a person might see a particular animal or bird, or object repeatedly, only to discover later that it has a significant meaning in their life. This event can be seen as a synchronistic event, providing a sense of connection and purpose in the person's life. This can be difficult to do if you don't understand how it works or how to work with it. In order to harness synchronicity as part of your life, here are some tips:

Be open-minded about your beliefs about reality—Don't get stuck in a rut where everything has an explanation and nothing happens by chance! There are plenty of things out there that science hasn't figured out yet; therefore, keep an open mind when exploring new ideas and experiences (and don't be afraid to let go of old ones).

> "*We found that trees could communicate, over the air and through their roots. Common sense hooted us down. We found that trees take care of each other. Collective science dismissed the idea. Outsiders discovered how seeds remember the seasons of their childhood and set buds accordingly. Outsiders discovered that trees sense the presence of other nearby life. That a tree learns to save water. That trees feed their young and synchronize their masts and bank resources and warn kin and send out signals to wasps to come and save them from attacks. "Here's a little outsider information, and you can wait for it to be confirmed. A forest knows things. They wire themselves up underground. There are brains down there, ones our own brains aren't shaped to see. Root plasticity, solving problems and making decisions. Fungal synapses. What else do you want to call it? Link enough trees together, and a forest grows aware.*
> *— Richard Powers, The Overstory*"

Remember that anything is possible—It doesn't matter if something seems impossible because chances are there's no rule against doing so! If someone tells me something won't work out for them because "it never has before," then I'm going right ahead into making sure those same things happen again just so they can see how wrong they were.

Therefore you can consider synchronicity as a divine gift that we can all access to create meaningful coincidences in our lives. When you work with synchronicity, you will find that there are many ways to connect with the divine and recognize synchronicity.

The Following Are Examples Of How This Can Happen:

- You may have an idea for something you want to do or make, but then suddenly someone gives it to you as a gift (or vice versa). This is because they have been inspired by God's guidance through their own intuition; they were able to see what was missing from your life without realizing it until they saw your desire come into being before their eyes!
- Your favorite song comes on at exactly the right moment when nothing else could have suited your mood better than listening right now.

Synchronicity and The Spiritual Dimension

The spiritual aspects of synchronicity are many and varied. Carl Jung believed that by recognizing the spiritual dimension of synchronicity, we can better understand our place in the universe. He also thought that prayer and meditation could help us tap into this power on a regular basis.

The idea that there is a spiritual side to our lives is not new; many religions have long held similar beliefs about God's involvement with our daily lives. The spiritual dimension of synchronicity is a complex one, as Jung himself noted. We can say that synchronicities happen because they are meant to happen; they are part of an overall plan for our lives (or perhaps even all life) that has been laid out beforehand by some higher power or principle beyond our comprehension.

The spiritual dimension of synchronicity is best understood as a realm of reality that transcends our material world. It's a place where we can find meaning, purpose, and connection with other people. The experience of synchronicity may be difficult for some people because it challenges their belief system about how the world works; however, it can also be very liberating when we realize that there are forces at work beyond our control or understanding.

The key here is not necessarily whether you believe in these forces but rather how open-minded you are willing to become when faced with something unexpected or unusual happening around you. As you can see, there are many different ways to interpret a meaningful coincidence. It's up to you how you want to view them and what they mean for your life.

One of the most important things about coincidences is that they can help shape our spiritual beliefs and change our perspective on life in general.

For example, if someone who has been struggling with their faith finds out that their favorite author passed away on the same day as their grandmother did, this may cause them to start questioning whether or not there is an afterlife or some kind of higher power watching over us all (and maybe even orchestrating these events).

This type of experience could lead someone who was previously skeptical about spirituality into exploring it further—or even becoming more religious!

Similarly, if someone sees a sign from God while driving down the road one day and gets into an accident shortly after seeing it (or something similar), this could prompt him/her into believing that God was trying to tell him or something important through those signs but didn't want him getting distracted while driving so he prevented him from being able to pay attention until after he got home safely.

For Jung, spirituality was not just about belief in a higher power or adherence to a particular doctrine. It was a process of individuation, where individuals strive to become their true selves by integrating their conscious and unconscious aspects. Jung believed that the unconscious contained spiritual insights and that individuals could access these insights through dreams, fantasies, and other unconscious material.

Jung also believed that spirituality was closely linked to creativity. He argued that artistic expression was a form of spiritual practice and that artists were able to tap into the collective unconscious to create works that touched people's souls. Therefore, It's important to note that synchronicity is not just a theory, but a tool for spiritual growth. It can help you understand your life lessons, manifest your desires and find peace within yourself.

When we learn how to recognize synchronicities in our daily lives, we open ourselves up to new opportunities for personal growth and self-discovery. Spirituality is an important part of many people's lives and can help them find their purpose or direction in life. This can also lead to more fulfilling relationships with others who share their values and beliefs.

When you have a strong sense of self-worth and confidence as well as faith in something greater than yourself (like God), it makes it easier for others around you to feel comfortable opening up about themselves too!

Synchronicity And Our Connection To The Universe

Synchronicity is a phenomenon that connects us to the Universe, and it can help us understand our place in it. This connection can be felt through synchronicities that bring meaning to our lives and show us what we need to know at any given moment. It can also give us insight into ourselves and others, allowing us to see past appearances or facades so we can connect with people on a deeper level.

> "*We often dream about people from whom we receive a letter by the next post. I have ascertained on several occasions that at the moment when the dream occurred the letter was already lying in the post-office of the addressee.*
> *— C.G. Jung, Synchronicity: An Acausal Connecting Principle*"

Synchronicity helps you realize when you're on track toward your desires and goals—and when you're not—by showing up in unexpected ways at unexpected times (or vice versa). For example, You may find yourself thinking about someone who just texted you while they're sitting next to someone else at lunch; or maybe there's an ad for something related to what interests you on TV while watching an unrelated show; maybe even finding money lying around after having been worried about finances all day long!

CHAPTER XII

In The Paranormal

The paranormal is a topic that has long been explored by scientists and researchers. Many people believe in the existence of paranormal phenomena, such as ghosts, spirits, or other entities that cannot be explained by current scientific theories. However, synchronicity is often associated with these types of experiences because it can provide evidence for their existence. In fact, Jung believed that synchronicity can help us understand our own unconscious minds better by helping us understand how they interact with reality at large.

Jung saw it as a form of paranormal perception that went beyond the limitations of the rational mind. Jung saw synchronicity as evidence of the existence of the collective unconscious, which he believed was a universal repository of symbolic images and archetypes. Jung argued that synchronistic events were evidence of a "psychoid" realm that was neither purely physical nor purely psychic.

> "*All matter, including you and I, has rhythmic movement within it and our quest should be to create a proper rhythmic harmony within ourselves...you feel happy when you sit near an ocean because your vibrations try to synchronize with the frequency of the waves.*
> *— Ed Viswanathan, Am I A Hindu? The Hinduism Primer*"

He believed that this realm was connected to the world of archetypes and symbolic images, which were fundamental to human experience. Jung saw synchronicity as evidence of a larger universe at work—a universe that we cannot always see but one that can be felt through our experiences and emotions.

He believed that this otherworldly force guides us toward our highest good and helps us find meaning in our lives by connecting seemingly unrelated events together through patterns or symbols (i.e., dreams). He has mentioned all of these paranormal events and phenomena that he has experienced in his life in most of his finest work.

Synchronicity And The Law Of Attraction

The law of attraction is the idea that our thoughts and emotions have an effect on the world around us. It's been popularized by books like "The Secret", but it's been around for centuries. Synchronicity and the Law of Attraction are closely related. The Law of Attraction is based on the idea that things come into our life as a result of our thoughts, emotions, and activities.

It's a universal law or universal want that says like attracts like—so if you think about something often enough, it will eventually manifest itself in your life (whether or not you realize it). Synchronicity works in tandem with this principle by helping us recognize when we're attracting something into our lives through our own thoughts and feelings; then it helps us make space for those things by allowing them to come through so we can see them clearly.

> "*I get so breathless, when you call my name,*
> *I've often wondered, do you feel the same?*
> *There's a chemistry, energy, a synchronicity*
> *When we're all alone.*
> *— Corinne Bailey Rae*"

That way we can take action on what's been attracted rather than having to wait around until another opportunity comes along later down the road! In fact, Jung believed that when we focus on something with strong emotions or intent, our thoughts will eventually manifest as reality—and vice versa: if you wish for something hard enough, it'll happen!

This is because everything happens at once—there are no isolated moments in time; everything exists simultaneously as part of a larger pattern called "synchronicity." So if you want something badly enough and put all your energy into making it happen...you might just get lucky!

Synchronicity And The Power Of Belief

Synchronicity is a powerful force, and it's not just for the lucky few. The more you believe in the universe and your ability to create your own reality, the more synchronicities you'll experience. When we think about our deepest desires—those things that would make us truly happy—and then go about manifesting them, we're tapping into this universal energy field.

> *"I'm at my strongest when I'm able to let go, when I suspend my beliefs as well as disbeliefs and leave myself open to all possibilities. That also seems to be when I'm able to experience the most internal clarity and synchronicities.*
> *— Anita Moorjani, Dying to Be Me: My Journey from Cancer, to Near Death, to True Healing"*

It's like putting out an intention into the world: "I want X." And then when something happens that brings us closer to getting what we want (like finding someone who shares similar interests), it feels like magic because of how aligned it is with our goal. But if we don't believe in synchronicity or our ability to manifest things through intentionality and actionable steps were taken toward achieving those goals, then these occurrences may seem random or coincidental instead of evidence that things are working out according to plan!

CHAPTER XIII

Benefits And Limitations

Benefits Of The Power Of Synchronistic Events in Our Lives

The key point is the more aware you become of synchronistic events in your life, the more likely it is that they will occur in the future. Synchronicity is a powerful force in our lives. It can help us find the answers we need and provide guidance when we're lost, but it's also something that can be difficult to understand.

> "*So perhaps happiness is synchronizing one's personal delusions of meaning with the prevailing collective delusions. As long as my personal narrative is in line with the narratives of the people around me, I can convince myself that my life is meaningful, and find happiness in that conviction.*
> *— Yuval Noah Harari, Sapiens: A Brief History of Humankind*"

Synchronicities are not always pleasant; sometimes they can be quite disturbing or even frightening (as evidenced by some of Jung's own experiences). The power of synchronicity lies in its ability to bring together seemingly unrelated events or people into one meaningful experience. These experiences can open up new possibilities for you and teach you about yourself at the same time!

Here Are Some Ways That Synchronicity Has Helped Others:

- It helped them overcome obstacles by showing them how everything happens for a reason (and therefore there are no coincidences).
- It helped them find solutions they didn't expect by making them look at problems from different angles than usual—and those new perspectives led directly toward solutions
- It can help you explore your purpose in life and find meaning in what you do. The more we understand about ourselves, the better equipped we are to make choices that align with our values and goals.
- Synchronicity also helps us become more mindful of our thoughts and actions so that we don't fall into old patterns that no longer serve us well—or even actively work against our best interests. When we are aware of these patterns, it gives us an opportunity to change them by making different choices going forward.
- Synchronicity is a powerful tool for self-reflection. It can help you to see the signs that your unconscious mind is sending you, and it can also help you to understand what those signs mean. By being open to the possibilities of synchronicity in your life, you'll be able to make sense of seemingly random events and find meaning in them—which will ultimately lead to personal growth.

It suggests that there are other principles at work in the universe that we do not fully understand. Synchronicity implies that there is a deeper, more profound reality that goes beyond what we can perceive with our five senses.

The Beauty Of Synchronicity In Our Life

Synchronicity can have a profound impact on our lives. Synchronicity is beautiful and interesting because it can have psychological effects on people. For example, you may find yourself feeling more optimistic about your life after experiencing a meaningful coincidence. This is because when we experience these coincidences, our brains interpret them as signs that everything is going to be okay and that there's some sort of higher power at work in our lives.

In addition to being good for your mental health, synchronicity may also have implications for society at large: it could help us improve our relationships with others and make us feel less alone in the world. Jung was interested in exploring the relationship between the psyche and the external world, and he believed that there was a deeper, underlying order to the universe that could be revealed through synchronistic events.

For example, a person may have a dream about a snake, and then later that day encounter a real snake while walking in the woods. This connection may reveal something about the person's inner psyche or their relationship to the natural world. One real-life example of synchronicity involves the composer Wolfgang Amadeus Mozart. According to legend, Mozart had a dream in which he heard a complete musical composition.

When he woke up, he was able to remember the entire composition and write it down. The composition was the opening of his Symphony №41, which is now known as the "Jupiter" Symphony. This is a powerful example of synchronicity, as it suggests a meaningful connection between Mozart's inner psyche and the external world of music. Another real-life example of synchronicity involves the novelist C.S. Lewis. Lewis was a deeply religious man who struggled with the death of his wife, Joy Davidman.

After her death, Lewis began to experience a series of coincidences that seemed to suggest a deeper spiritual meaning. For example, he received a letter from a fan of his work who was also named Joy, and later met a woman named Helen Joy who shared many of his wife's qualities. These synchronistic events helped Lewis to find comfort and meaning in his grief and inspired him to write.

Implications of Synchronicity

Synchronicity challenges us to look beyond traditional notions of causality and consider the possibility that events may be connected in ways that we do not understand. When we experience synchronistic events, we may feel a sense of awe or wonder at the mysterious connections that seem to be at work in our lives.

> "*Things began happening with odd synchronicity, as if the universe itself was conspiring on behalf of their love story.*
> *— John Mark Green*"

For example, if we get a promotion at work, we might attribute it to our hard work and dedication. However, synchronicity suggests that there may be other factors at play, such as the timing of the promotion or the people we meet along the way.

For example, if two people meet at a random event and discover that they have shared interests or experiences, this could lead to a deeper connection between them. Synchronicity can also help us understand the connections between our own inner worlds and the inner worlds of others, leading to greater empathy, compassion, and a greater appreciation for the beauty and complexity of life.

> "*Intuition goes before you, showing you the way. Emotion follows behind, to let you know when you go astray. Listen to your inner voice. It is the calling of your spiritual GPS system seeking to keep you on track towards your true destiny.*
> *— Anthon St. Maarten, Divine Living: The Essential Guide To Your True Destiny*"

Synchronicity Is A Very Emotional Event

Synchronicity represents an underlying psychological truth about our subjective experiences of the world. He believed synchronicity is an attempt by the unconscious to communicate with consciousness and that the way synchronicities were interpreted could lead to spiritual enlightenment. The relationship between synchronicity and stress is one area of interest, as it has been found that experiencing a high level of synchronicity can help reduce stress levels.

Criticism of Jung's Theory

Despite its many supporters, Jung's theory of synchronicity has also faced criticism from skeptics and mainstream scientists. One of the main criticisms is that synchronicity is a subjective phenomenon that cannot be objectively verified. Skeptics argue that synchronistic events can be explained by chance or selective attention and that there is no evidence to support the existence of a psychoid realm.

> "*But are the twin souls destined to be together? Synchronicity is at work here to bring the two back together again. How entrancing to find the same magical alchemy still at work, just as it was at the first meeting – a recognition of a deep rooted love so entrenched and so accepted, it could only have been forged in other lifetimes together. And probably that is what love at first sight is, recognition of an ancient love.*
> *— Chimnese Davids, My Unrequited Love Letters*"

The concept of synchronicity has been criticized as being too vague or unmeasurable by some scientists who reject its validity, but it remains popular with many people who find it useful in understanding their own experiences with coincidence and pattern recognition.

The Limitations of Jung's Theory

Jung's theories are difficult to empirically test, and this makes it difficult for us to know if they're true. Theoretical bias is also a concern: Jung may have been biased by his own experiences, or he may have been influenced by other theorists who were also biased. Finally, there's the danger of misinterpretation. Some people might think that Jung meant something different than what he actually said—and this might lead individuals astray when attempting to implement his ideas in their own life.

> "*We all have a soul family, the ones that ignite and support our truth. They feed something in us we weren't aware we needed before them. They'll make you face yourself and become raw and authentic. You'll roam but never too far from eachother for the invisible thread of connectedness; once opened can never be locked. They are the ones who will see you through all the important days of your life no matter what tributes and trials you face. They'll just be there, in presence, in synchronicity or in spirit.*
> *— Nikki Rowe*"

CHAPTER XIV

Final Thoughts

About Author

Enter Caption

Mr. Som Dutt lives Philosophy and Psychology by heart. When he was studying M.Tech at IIT, he got deeply indulged in the subject and started reading Friedrich Nietzsche. Such experience gave wings to his curiosity.

He is the Top Writer on Philosophy and Psychology on Medium.com and has written over 700 articles. He has written many viral articles and has more than 10K followers. He is making a 6-figure income with writing. I make people think, relate, feel & move.

Follow him on Social Media and get up to date with his new articles and books.

Instagram: @somdutt_freespirita
Medium: somdutt777
Gmail: somdutt777@gmail.com
Twitter: som_dutt_
Linkedin: som-dutt-950472b7

www.ingramcontent.com/pod-product-compliance
Ingram Content Group UK Ltd.
Pitfield, Milton Keynes, MK11 3LW, UK
UKHW041820200726
13854UKWH00001BA/144